Abby Ravenscroft
Illustrations by Ella Connolly

Sistersaurus!

Bumblebee Books
London

BUMBLEBEE PAPERBACK EDITION

Copyright © Abby Ravenscroft 2021
Illustrations by Ella Connolly

A CIP catalogue record for this title is
available from the British Library.

ISBN: 978-1-83934-231-8

Bumblebee Books is an imprint of
Olympia Publishers.

First Published in 2021

Bumblebee Books
Tallis House
2 Tallis Street
London
EC4Y 0AB

Printed in Great Britain

www.olympiapublishers.com

Dedication

For my three little girls, may this story always bring you smiles and giggles.

Our little sister
is VERY noisy.

Mummy says she is a sistersaurus!

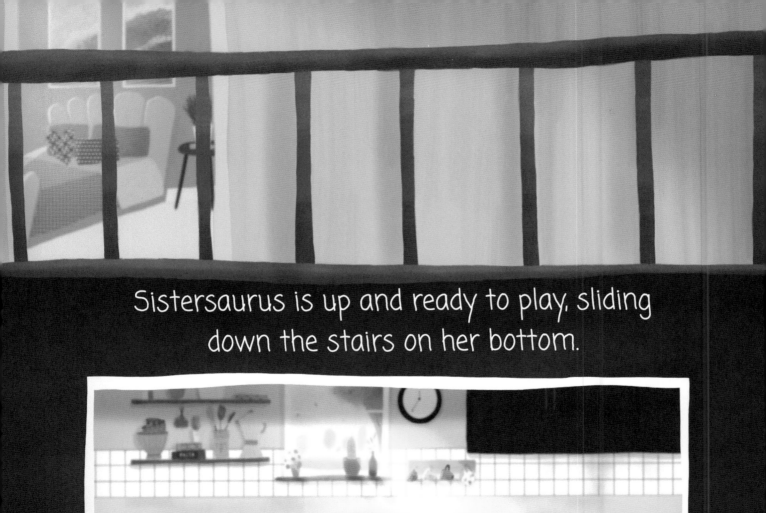

Sistersaurus is up and ready to play, sliding down the stairs on her bottom.

Mummy is always chasing her around the house, she can run so fast it can be hard to catch her. Sometimes she can be clumsy and knock things over.

CRASH

CLATTER

SMASH!

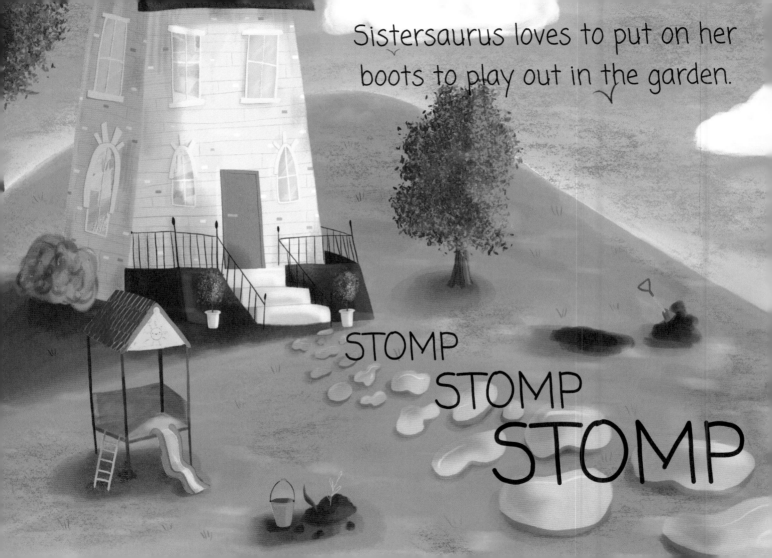

Sistersaurus loves to put on her boots to play out in the garden.

STOMP
STOMP
STOMP

Digging for bugs and chasing butterflies.

She doesn't even mind if she gets messy.

Sistersaurus is always hungry, her favourite is when
Mummy bakes cakes.

Sometimes, she even pinches our
food when we aren't looking!

CRUNCH

CHOMP

SLURP

When we watch our favourite cartoons, sistersaurus can never sit still and laughs as loud as can be.

GIGGLE

WRIGGLE

GIGGLE

Bath time is the best! Sistersaurus takes her ducks for a swim and covers them in bubbles. But Mummy gets cross when she leaves puddles on the floor.

SPLISH

SPLASH

SPLOSH

When the stars come out and it is time for bed, the house gets very quiet.

Mummy has rocked her straight to sleep,
she doesn't make a sound.

ove our little sistersaurus, even when she's loud.

About the Author

Abby Ravenscroft grew up in North Devon with her parents and two siblings. The family then moved to Hampshire when she was in her early teens. Abby has continued living in Hampshire where she shares a home with her partner and three daughters, who have given her the inspiration to relight her childhood dream of writing books for children.

Printed in Great Britain
by Amazon